English text and book design by Kristine Brogno and Jessica Dacher.
Typeset in Aunt Mildred and Chanson D'Amour.
Printed in China.

Library of Congress Cataloging-in-Publication Data available.
ISBN 0-8118-2526-4

Distributed in Canada by Raincoast Books
8680 Cambie Street, Vancouver, British Columbia V6P 6M9

10 9 8 7 6 5 4 3 2 1

Chronicle Books
85 Second Street, San Francisco, California 94105

www.chroniclebooks.com/Kids

For Adrien

Isabelle and the Angel

by Thierry Magnier • illustrated by Georg Hallensleben

chronicle books · san francisco

Isabelle lived alone and she was bored.
She wanted to live and learn and...eat.
Isabelle liked to eat. Sometimes she ate
a little too much. But it was so good!

Isabelle liked
to play with her food too.
She made pretty paintings with
pink cake and strawberry jam.
Sometimes it was a bit messy.
But it was so fun!

What Isabelle liked best was going to the Museum.
She went every day. There, she sat in a red velvet chair...

and she gazed at her favorite painting.
For in this painting lived...

the little Angel.

One day
Isabelle
heard a voice.

It was the little Angel!

"Why do you come to the Museum every day?" he asked.

"Because," said Isabelle.

"Because why?" asked the little Angel.

Before Isabelle could answer, the little Angel played her a sweet song on his trumpet. Isabelle turned even pinker with delight.

Then the little Angel said, "follow me." And he took Isabelle on a special tour of the Museum.

It was their secret.

Isabelle liked all the things
the little Angel showed her,

all except for one...

the Lovely Statue.

"Isn't she lovely?" asked the little Angel.

Suddenly Isabelle felt very small.

"Why don't you like the Lovely Statue?" asked the little Angel.

"Because," said Isabelle.

"Because why?" asked the little Angel.

"Because I like you!" said Isabelle.

The little Angel kissed Isabelle on the cheek.

Isabelle knew the little Angel could never leave the Museum. She missed her friend when she was not with him.

She missed him so much
that the next day when she
went to the Museum...

she decided she would stay.

Now, Isabelle is the Guardian of the Museum.

She keeps an eye on things.

And the little Angel
keeps an eye on her.